Kites

Written by ᴊᴏ ...

MW01032378

CONTENTS

Rigby

Kitesurfing

Kitesurfing is one of the fastest-growing sports in the world.

Kitesurfers use the energy of the wind to rush across the water on a board attached to a controllable kite. They are participants in a challenging sport full of thrills and excitement.

To be able to jump, jibe, and ride in the air across the water, a kitesurfer needs to have some special gear.

Kites

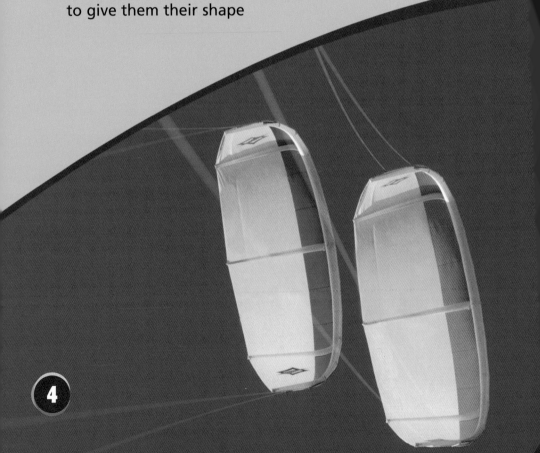

Kitesurfers can use different types of kites.

Some of these kites are:
- inflated tube kites, which are easy to launch and relaunch from the water
- single skin kites that are built around a frame
- ram-air foil kites that are filled by the wind to give them their shape

Boards

Kitesurfers can use different types of boards.

Two types of boards are:

• directional kiteboards – especially designed for kiteboarding (These have foot straps, fins, and sometimes footpads.)

• wakeboards – designed to be pulled behind boats for tricks and jumps (Only a confident kitesurfer usually uses a wakeboard.)

Wakeboard

Directional kiteboard

Harness

A harness allows the surfer to be connected to the kite. A kite has strong flying lines that are connected to a control bar. The control bar has a loop that can fit into the hook of the harness.

The hook helps to prevent the kitesurfer's arms from getting too tired, by taking the *pull* of the kite.

The surfer can use the harness like a power control system to increase or decrease power during kitesurfing.

Optional Accessories to wear

Wearing the correct equipment is important for the safety of the kitesurfer.

Wetsuits, buoyancy jackets, helmets, sunglasses, hook-knives, and booties can often be found in the kitesurfer's kit.

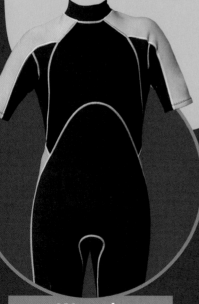

Wetsuit
Helps to keep the kitesurfer warm.

Buoyancy jacket
Helps to keep the kitesurfer afloat.

Sunglasses
Protects the kitesurfer's eyes from bright light.

Helmet
Helps to prevent any serious head injuries.

Hook-knife
Can be used to cut tangled lines.

Booties
Can be used for warmth and protection.

The Art of Kitesurfing

Like any flying or sailing sport, it is best to have a steady, constant wind. Kitesurfing gear is made to fly in winds as low as 8 knots and as high as 50 knots. Once the kite is airborne, the surfer is pulled along the surface of the water by the power of the wind collecting in the large kite.

With this wind power, the surfer can steer, jump, and land. Learning to kitesurf takes a lot of practice and persistence to get it right.

Some extreme surfers have surfed in winds up to 75 knots.

Many kitesurfers can learn how to kiteboard on land before venturing out into the water. They choose an area with wide open spaces and no obstructions.

Kiteboarders should wear as much "body armor" as they can, to prevent any injuries.

wind window

Downwind

Wind

The air space in which a kite can fly is called a "wind window." When the kite is directly above the surfer's head, it is in the neutral position and has less pull.

As the kite is steered from one direction to the other, it passes through the "power zone."

Kitesurfing in the power zone is full of thrills, and can be very fast and dangerous.

A kitesurfer can use the flying lines to slow down, speed up, and to steer.

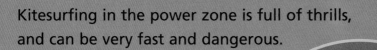

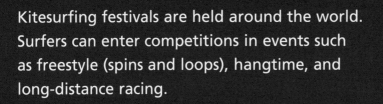

Kitesurfing festivals are held around the world. Surfers can enter competitions in events such as freestyle (spins and loops), hangtime, and long-distance racing.

A surfer needs to understand weather and wind conditions and the surrounding environment that he or she is going to surf in.

Kitesurfing is not as dangerous as some sports, but safety has to be taken seriously. Respect should always be shown to others, and kitesurfers need to know and follow certain rules.

Rules

- Stay clear of electrical power lines and overhead obstructions.

- Choose a safe launching site.

- Have a competent launching assistant to help you.

- Always announce when you are launching your kite.

- Keep outsiders outside your "wind window."

- Do not let your kite lines cross anyone's path.

- Disable unattended kites.

- Surfers sailing forward, with the wind blowing from the right, have the right of way.

Index

Explanation

How to write an explanation:

Step One

- Choose a topic.
- Make a list of the things you know about the topic.
- Write down the things you need to find out.

Explanations explain how things work and why things happen.

Topic:
Kitesurfing

What I know:
We need wind to be able to kitesurf.
Kitesurfing can be dangerous.
You need a board and a kite to be able to kitesurf.

Research:
I need to find out:

What kinds of kites and boards are there?
What other equipment does a kitesurfer need?
How do you kitesurf?
What are the rules for kitesurfing?

Step Two

- Research the things you need to know.
- You can go to the library, use the Internet, or ask an expert.
- Make notes.

Step Three

- Organize the information.
- Make some headings.

Safety Gear for the Kitesurfer

- wetsuit
- buoyancy jacket
- helmet
- sunglasses
- hook-knife
- booties

Boards

- Kitesurfers use different types of boards.
- Directional kiteboards – foot straps, fins, and footpads
- Wakeboards – pulled behind boats for tricks and jumps

Step Four

Use your notes to write your explanation. You can use:

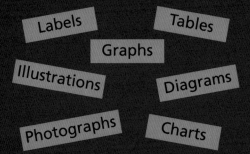

Labels

Tables

Graphs

Illustrations

Diagrams

Photographs

Charts

Your explanation could have...

... a contents page

CONTENTS

... an index

Index

Some explanations also have a glossary to explain difficult words.

19

Guide Notes

Title: **Kitesurfing**
Stage: Fluency (3)

Text Form: Informational Explanation
Approach: Guided Reading
Processes: Thinking Critically, Exploring Language, Processing Information
Written and Visual Focus: Informational Explanation, Illustrative Diagram

THINKING CRITICALLY
(sample questions)

Before Reading – Establishing Prior Knowledge
• What do you know about kitesurfing?

Visualizing the Text Content
• What might you expect to see in this book?
• What form of writing do you think will be used by the author?
Look at the contents page and index. Encourage the children to think about the information and make predictions about the text content.

After Reading – Interpreting the Text
• In what ways do you think this sport is challenging and demanding?
• What skills do you think are necessary for this sport? Why?
• What do you know about kitesurfing that you didn't know before?
• What things in the book helped you understand the information?
• What questions do you have after reading the text?

EXPLORING LANGUAGE

Terminology
Photograph credits, index, contents page, imprint information, ISBN number

Vocabulary
Clarify: participant, jibe, launch, confident, harness, optional, accessories, kit, constant, persistence, venturing, knots, challenging
Focus the children's attention on **adjectives, homonyms, antonyms,** and **synonyms** if appropriate.